The Mermaid and the River Otter: A Fable

The Fable Triad

CS Simpson

Published by CSS Stories, 2023.

THE MERMAID AND THE RIVER OTTER: A FABLE

First edition. February 24, 2023.

Copyright © 2023 CS Simpson.

ISBN: 979-8215487303

Written by CS Simpson.

Table of Contents

For my in-laws, Junior and Kay

*"Words have no wings
but they can fly a thousand miles."*

~ *Korean Proverb*

*"We can't heal the world today
but we can begin with a voice of compassion,
a heart of love, an act of kindness."*

~ *Mary Davis, Author*

STORY INTRODUCTION

CREATED FOR ADULT READERS, *The Mermaid and the River Otter* is a new tale told in an old writing style. I grew up with a copy of Rudyard Kipling's *Just So Stories* (from 1902) and was fascinated by his strange accounts of the supposed origins of unusual creatures and language, talking animals in a non-picture book, and his clever use of language to make an important point. I wrote this story with the idea of creating a similarly timeless tale and to remind us all of the need for social courtesy in a gentle way.

In order to set the book apart from most commercial stories, I've chosen to write my fables with an intentional lack of contractions, as well as deliberate repetitions of both phrases and ideas. These repetitions are meant to draw the reader into an ancient kind of suspended reality, reinforce a concept, and even give the story its own poetic rhythm.

Likewise, I chose the intentional use of lists in sets of threes, including the final tally of this book series—The Fable Triad. Many cultures revere triads because they're seen as having a beginning, a middle, and an end—creating a sense of completeness.

Each character's name is based on the area of the globe where scientists think these creatures may have originated, and I've included a pronunciation guide at the back of the book for those who are interested. The tale is set "many, many moons ago, before countless humans roamed the Earth," so the intention is meant to show (perhaps) that mankind adopted these names, with the character's dominating personalities, into their respective languages over time. It's also meant to show how immense and varied our world is, yet we all have a common beginning; a common existence; body, mind, and spirit.

My fables are unique in that they each have several morals interwoven within the narrative, instead of the classic idea of ending the story with a single intended teaching. The lessons represented in these stories are age-old, yet still timely for every culture.

Though each of my fables are separate tales with separate characters, they're meant to embody the same global time frame and can be read in any order. They begin almost identically, much like Kipling's *Just So Stories*, in order to set the tone and rhythm as complementary to the other two. But—worry not! *The Elephant and the Dragon*, *The Dolphin and the Octopus*, and *The Mermaid and the River Otter* each offer their own unique accounts and don't follow the exact same pattern throughout.

I welcome readers of any age, and even hope that parents think of this story as a family book— perhaps one to be read aloud and discussed together.

Enjoy!

  – CS Simpson

CHAPTER 1

MANY, MANY MOONS AGO, before countless humans roamed the Earth, a mermaid and a river otter supervised The Tidal Realm together in a sheltered coastal lagoon called Counselor's Cove. They were both calm, loving, and smart leaders who tried to share their wisdom with their fellow tidal area creatures.

The glittery female mermaid, named Corinna (which means "maiden" in Greek), was known as *The Mindful Merwoman*. Her tanned upper body was smooth and free from scales with two human-like arms. Her lower half resembled a long green-blue fish's tail, yet ended in a translucent, dolphin-sized fluke. She wore a woven seagrass band across her chest and an abandoned sea shell in her long purplish-blue hair. Possessing both gills and lungs, she was a swift underwater swimmer who also loved to sunbathe on the lagoon's many boulders. Corinna governed her fellow creatures with a kind heart and a unique sense of understanding.

The dark brown male river otter, named Tonino (which means "priceless one" or "highly praiseworthy" in Italian), was known as *The Kindly Little King*. His streamlined, muscular body was covered in short, dense black-brown fur, with a slightly lighter shade on his belly. His feet were webbed for easy, agile swimming. Tonino's long tail was thick and powerful, perfect for both steering and propulsion in the water. His short muzzle was whiskered, with small ears set on either side of his weasel-like head. Tonino governed with kindness and a sense of solemnity.

The estuary residents respected this particular pair of tidal counselors for their communication, empathy, and motivational skills. Choosing to govern others is a very great responsibility, so they held this power very carefully.

The mermaid and the river otter lived inside a large coastal inlet carved into the Earth's single landmass called Counselor's Cove. On two long sides of this lagoon, sun-warmed beaches led up to a dense inland rainforest. A third side held a cobblestone shoreline at the base of tall lichen-coated rocky cliffs, and the fourth side contained a series of submerged sandbars, which acted like natural gates into the open ocean. These sandbars allowed the planet's tidal force to change the depth of the estuary twice a day. Because of this unique mix of environments,

Counselor's Cove included several well-known habitats in one big, diverse area. It was filled with temperate water interspersed by reeds and groups of chunky boulders and smooth rocks.

The deepest waters near the outer sandbars held a vast kelp forest, thick sea lettuce beds, and sandy floors. Closer to shore, there were salty tidal marshes covered in bright green pickleweed succulents, tall grass-like sedges, flowering rushes, and the ever-popular cattail. Twisty mangrove trees dipped their lacy roots into the salty waters closest to shore and created a protected nursery for fish, jellyfish, and sharks alike. The warm, shallow places that lay between low and high tides were perfect for feathery red algae, slimy green seaweed, and eelgrass meadows. A long sandy shore was dotted with several kinds of beach grasses, tall reeds, lanky palm trees, and more twisty mangrove trees. Further inland, a forest of fast-growing bamboo flourished near various palm trees, tall Brazil nut trees, rubber trees, and more. This coastal rainforest formed a thick green wall around the estuary and its inhabitants. Thankfully, no additional food or supplies needed to be brought into the area from elsewhere, because the space was its own natural ecosystem.

A great variety of marine, amphibious, and land species lived peacefully together inside and around Counselor's Cove. The strange mixture of fresh and salt water made for a very specific kind of habitat, which attracted unique critters. There were scuttling crayfish, numerous wary crabs, and long-legged water birds who enjoyed the warming waters of the tidal zone. Walking mudskipper fish, water-spitting archer fish, noisy frogs, and harmless nurse sharks nestled in amongst the mangrove roots. Lumbering alligators, curious turtles, territorial muskrats, and barking sea lions traveled between the deep and shallow spaces with ease. And there were colorful parrots, slow-grazing manatees, and mischievous merfolk who lived in the waters near the sandbars. The lagoon even had a tree-covered island in the middle where lemurs and monkeys screeched and played together day and night. Due to the incredible diversity gathered in the warm, brackish waters, there was quite a variety of temporary communities scattered around the area. Each encampment was suited best for the individual species, so there were nests on the sand, dens in the rocks, and schools in the seaweed and marshes.

Each day, new fish, birds, aquatic mammals, and reptiles came to Counselor's Cove to speak with the mermaid and the river otter, hoping to discuss a wide variety of topics. Some came for advice on how to resolve a heated dispute between family, friends, or neighbors. Some sought a new direction in life, or inquired about how to choose a mate. There were also some who came only to thank the counselors for the way they had advised The Tidal Realm thus far, and perhaps ask for a blessing.

These temporary visitors to the estuary were known as seekers. Seekers journeyed to the busy Counselor's Cove from their homes along every sandy seashore, darkened crevice, thick seagrass bed, cozy shore den, and every place in between. Those who were able to swim arrived to speak with the lagoon counselors faster and easier than those who needed to walk or crawl (of course). But do not worry for those who were born, or hatched, without fins or flippers. There were numerous well-maintained paths both underwater and across the sandy shores of the lagoon for the slow-moving creatures, allowing seekers to enjoy the company of their fellow travelers along the way.

When a seeker arrived inside the estuary, they would first check in with one of the meticulous watchers (you will learn more about them shortly) who kept track of each arrival. Once checked in, the visitors would choose a place to stay for a night or two. There were many options for occupying their time while waiting for their turn to talk with the counselors. They could swim among the mangrove roots along the water's edge and explore the many mazes. Or they could play in the underwater meadow of seagrass, or sunbathe on the sand, or play in the rainforest along the edge of the lagoon while visiting with other compatible species.

Each morning, just before the sun cracked the horizon, Corinna and Tonino would meet at the Guidance Rocks, a closely situated pair of boulders in the shallow part of the lagoon. These rocks were a little underwater when the tide was high, yet above the waterline when the tide was low. The pair of boulders had a nearby sand berm (or narrow stretch of sand) essentially connecting them to the shore. This natural arrangement made the two boulders the perfect place for the pair to meet with either the water-breathing species or the air-breathing species.

Before coastal messengers brought the first seekers of the day to the counselors, the leaders of the Tidal Realm were usually able to have a quick conversation. Most of them went something like this:

"Good day, Tonino. Were your evening hours agreeable?" Corinna the mermaid might say to her fellow counselor.

"Yes, of course," the river otter might answer. "I joined a fun dancing party on the beach for a while until a driving rain convinced us all to go home. I am grateful my den in the sandbank kept me dry and warmed me up. What about your evening?"

"It was peaceful. I was not aware it had rained all night until I surfaced a little while ago," the mermaid might answer. "The waters on the ocean side floor of the estuary were calm for my husband and me until the busyness of the early morning began."

Tonino might sigh a small river otter sigh and say something like, "I wish I was able to breathe both air and water like you can, my amphibious friend. To spend a night below the waters, being rocked to sleep by the currents where the wind, rain, and tide do not disturb would be a lovely thing, I think."

"Yes, I believe you would enjoy your extended time underwater if you could, my friend," Corinna might answer. "You seem to love visiting with everyone you meet, and more time with the water-breathers would probably be your kind of party."

But soon enough, coastal messengers would lead the first seekers of the morning up to the mermaid and the river otter and they would officially begin their day. Each seeker (or group of seekers) was allowed a private audience with either the mermaid or the river otter, and given as much time as was deemed necessary to resolve an issue or a question. The still-waiting seekers lined up beside each boulder and visited quietly with each other until it was their turn to speak with the counselors.

Corinna and Tonino spent most of their hours listening to the questions and concerns of those who had traveled across the lagoon to speak with them. They both did their best to help their fellow intertidal creatures by answering questions truthfully and resolving disputes calmly.

In the moments just before dawn and before dusk, the mermaid and the river otter reserved time for the nocturnal seekers. They did not want to leave any nighttime critters out of the process simply because their bodies required a different relationship with the path of the sun than most. So, the counselors stayed in place, sitting on their respective boulders until twilight, when it was time for the evening patrol to begin their shift.

When the last of the light had disappeared behind the edge of the tallest of the sand dunes, when the frogs and shore birds began their evening songs, the counselors told the seekers still gathered by the boulders that they would see them in the morning.

Then the mermaid and the river otter made their way to their respective safe havens on opposite ends of the estuary. Corinna swam to her underwater sea cave near the protected lagoon's end and slept on a soft bed of seaweed with her new husband, Zamir (which means "beautiful voice" or "the song" in Hebrew). Tonino swam to shore, shook the water from his oily coat, and entered his cozy bachelor-sized den carved into a tall, grassy sand hill near the mouth of the freshwater river.

So it was in this manner that each day passed beside the water in the diverse coastal estuary.

CHAPTER 2

A S YOU MIGHT IMAGINE, the daily work of advising the various inhabitants of The Tidal Realm could take a toll on its dedicated counselors. Therefore, the mermaid and the river otter were not perpetually available to meet with seekers.

A wise old owl from a previous era, had advised his own set of Animal Kingdom governors (which happened to be a tortoise and a raven back then) to reserve personal time for themselves in order to avoid becoming worn out from such a heavy social responsibility. A messenger pigeon had shared this information with the Tidal Realm's leaders in those days (who happened to be a stork and a manatee), and they had chosen to follow this wisdom as well. So, it had been decided that every new moon cycle, when the sky was dark for four nights without moonlight shining down on the lagoon, the reigning leaders should take several private hours away from the many seekers' questions and arguments. It was meant to be a time to refresh, meditate, and enjoy their families; a time to play, learn, and rest; a time to feed their weary souls.

So, when Corinna the mermaid was not working, she loved to spend her time exploring the sandbar-clogged mouth of the estuary with members of her pod. She often searched for discarded shells or sat on a lagoon boulder and sang with the other merfolk. Corinna spent the evenings with her husband

Zamir, where they were still creating a customized home for themselves out of various rocks, shells, and seaweed. Whereas Tonino the river otter (as you might also imagine) preferred to sunbathe with his fellow otters on the warm beach sand, or investigate the rocky crevices of the boulder piles, or nap contentedly in the shade of a tree. He spent his evenings alone, savoring the quiet. He would go over each day's conversations in his mind, while curled up in the warm, dry den he had carved out of the sandbank himself.

Now, the Earth was still quite young in those days. A vast superocean covered the globe and seated inside it was a massive supercontinent that had not yet been broken up by the planet's plate tectonics. The boundary between the opposing forces of land and water included tall cliffs, endless meandering shorelines, and many sea caves, bays, and gulfs. But Counselor's Cove was the largest of these inlets, by far. The Tidal Realm functioned as its own governing body, separate from either The Animal Kingdom of the supercontinent, or The Oceanic Empire of the superocean. The paths of these three governing bodies rarely crossed, although some of The Tidal Realm's inhabitants were able to cross into the domain of the other two.

At the time of this particular tale, no battles were being fought either inside or around the protected coastal lagoon. Wars between the assorted intertidal species were rare, though they did erupt occasionally. The various creatures of the earth, water, and sky were fortunate enough to have found a peaceful balance between need and want.

It should also be noted that there were still very few human beings in those days, though some had recently come to settle close to the warmer ocean climes. Thankfully, mankind had not yet attempted to reside near the brackish waters of Counselors Cove. However, the members of The Tidal Realm needed to be careful when venturing up on the surrounding shore, just in case. Every living creature either inside or around the waters could still travel wherever they wished—if given enough time, energy, and fortitude. And many did.

The mermaid and the river otter knew having many different kinds of semi-aquatic species in one place could eventually cause strife in some form or another. Given the long lines and diversity of visitors, there was great potential for frustration or confusion between the species waiting to speak with the counselors. For this reason, there was ever an attentive eye on duty, either sitting high in the trees or gliding on the breeze.

A great white pelican named Hamza (a name meaning "strong" or "steadfast" in Turkish) was one of the various aerial watchers who patrolled above the estuary and its bordering rainforest every day. He held the important job of watch commander, which meant he was in charge of the other watchers during their working hours. When he was on duty, he spread his black-tipped white wings and rode the warm air currents high above Counselor's Cove. From this elevated vantage-point, Hamza carefully tracked the movements of the inhabitants and reported anything unusual or concerning to his helper hummingbird. The hummingbird would then quickly take his messages down below to waiting sparrows since his voice was not loud.

The lagoon watchers came from a wide assortment of species. They all lived both within and around the brackish waters. There were rat, monkey, and panther watchers. There were duck, seagull, and egret watchers. And there were sea turtle, sea lion, and merfolk watchers. They all worked collectively to keep the gathered seekers tranquil and satisfied while they waited to speak with the mermaid or the river otter (as much as possible, that is).

Hamza had keen pelican eyesight and became distracted by schools of fish down below, so a flock of intermediary air watchers were always around to gently remind him about his duty. These faithful little hummingbirds were ever at the ready to relay Hamza's concerns to the appropriate nearby ground- or water-based watchers with chirps and twitters. The watchers, whether air-breather or water-breather, would then carefully draw near to the disturbance (or potential disturbance) and quietly observe until they understood the mood of the creature in question. After a moment's assessment, the watcher then approached the animal and offered his or her assistance.

It was in this manner that most serious confrontations were easily circumvented. It was also the reason there was still peace around the protected lagoon—even though it accommodated many diverse species which would not naturally get along.

When the duskiness of early twilight fell over the estuary and its rainforest, yet the sky was still lit with the last hours of daylight, the estuary's inhabitants made their way back to their own rest areas and their own families for the evening—except for the nocturnal ones, of course.

Twilight also signaled a changing of the guard from the daytime watchers to the night patrol. Included in these nocturnal creatures were: hooting owls, hand-washing raccoons, scuttling hermit crabs, scavenging catfish, duck-billed platypuses, island-hopping lemurs, and more. When only the moon shone its bluish light on the lagoon, these animals visited with each other, swapping stories.

Hamza the great white pelican would turn over his aerial lagoon patrol to Lalita the large fruit bat (whose name means "playful, charming, desirable" in Sanskrit). Hamza spent his time off hunting for food by catching it in his large gular pouch, playing with his newly hatched chicks, and roosting near his partner. Their home was a nest of sticks tucked into a rocky crevice on the cobblestone beach under the cliffs. Most of the lagoon watchers found private places away from the Guidance Rocks when they were not on duty, so they could relax without the noise of the lagoon. Like the other watchers, Hamza needed his home to be restful, peaceful, and private.

Do not forget about Hamza the great white pelican. We will check in on him again later in this story.

CHAPTER 3

ONE WINDY AUTUMN EVENING, as had happened several times before, a new nocturnal mammal had her chance to speak with Counselor Corinna. As the sun disappeared beneath the tall trees of the rainforest, a timid juvenile platypus used her beaver-like tail to swim up to the base of Guidance Rock.

Her name was Tambreet (a word which is an indigenous Australian name for the species), and she was nervous about asking the mermaid a personal question.

When Corinna saw the platypus pause at the base of her boulder, she dropped gently onto a shallowly submerged nearby rock so the seeker could introduce herself.

"Good day, Counselor Corinna," the dark brown platypus finally said. She settled herself on the same rock as the mermaid to keep her head out of the water. "I am called Tambreet and I am grateful you had time for me this evening."

The mermaid's long, purplish-blue hair fluttered in the breeze as she said, "Of course I have the time, my dear. And I am especially happy to make your acquaintance, Tambreet. I have not had the fortune of meeting many of your species, since your kind tends to keep to the freshwater rivers inside the rainforest."

The young platypus dipped her head bashfully, causing the tip of her flat snout to drop into the water. Tambreet pressed the tips of her clawed front feet together nervously under her body. "Yes, we do not come this far into the salty waters very often. I am here to ask for advice. It is not important, though. It is something . . . personal."

When Tambreet did not continue, Corinna pressed, "It is obviously important to *you*. How can I help?"

Tambreet raised her leathery snout out of the water to look at the mermaid before continuing. "Well, you see, my brother and sister and I do not have many friends. I was wondering if you could help us figure out what we have been doing wrong."

Corinna was surprised at this. The young mammal in front of her seemed good-natured and easy to speak with. "The other platypuses do not find you or your siblings agreeable?"

"Oh, they do," Tambreet said, flustered. "We have friends among our fellow platypuses, but I want *other* friends. I try to be kind to the many creatures of the rainforest, like monkeys and toucans and frogs—especially the monkeys because I like how they can swing. But the way everyone leaves soon after I arrive makes it clear they do not want to be around me. I was hoping you had some hints on how to start conversations with other species. It seems easy enough for you to do."

"I can certainly share a few ideas," Counselor Corinna said. "Tell me a little more about your difficulties making friends."

"It is just that no one, besides platypuses that is, wants to talk or swim with me for long. Either that or they soon make fun of me, and I leave on my own."

"Tambreet, I am sad to hear this," Corinna answered with a frown. "Those who make fun of you must not have good manners."

"I think it is just the way we platypuses look. Why, just the other day, I was trying to play with a couple of beavers and they teased me about the fine fur that covers my tail. I know their tails are wide and flat like mine, but just because mine has fur, and theirs does not, should not be a reason to avoid being my friend."

As any lingering light from the sky above disappeared completely, and the waters became as dark as the night itself, the counselor tried an indirect approach. "It is true," Corinna said. "You have some similarities to the beavers, but you are not a beaver. They should not expect you to look like them."

Tambreet's flat snout bobbed up and down as she nodded, though Corinna could barely see. "That is what I said! 'We both love to swim and eat and live in warm, cozy dens,' I told them. But it seems beavers do not like to talk much because they left. I have not managed to make any beaver friends yet."

"Well, that is unfortunate." Corinna twirled her hair around a finger while she thought of another creature with features similar to a platypus. "Your beautiful snout—though soft and flexible—is so like a duck's bill. Have you tried to make friends with any of the many species of ducks?"

"Yes," Tambreet responded. "I have approached various ducks a few times. But as soon as I swim up to say hello, they fly away. I must startle them by swimming too fast. I have not managed to make friends among any of the bird species yet."

"Hmm." Sensing she may have asked too many questions, Corinna decided to change the angle of the conversation. "My dear Tambreet, you are a beautiful and extraordinary animal of land, freshwater, and saltwater, and you bring a very special something to our protected lagoon. I am sure others would like you if they simply spent the time to get to know you. I suppose your unusual look may intimidate some creatures."

"But I am a platypus. We have *always* looked this way. We are meant to look *exactly* this way." Tambreet appeared truly confused in the feeble moonlight.

The mermaid secured a few strands of wind-blown hair behind an ear before answering. "Yes, I agree. Your shiny fur, flat fuzzy tail, and soft flexible snout are all perfect for a platypus. However, your particular combination of features is quite exceptional. No other lagoon inhabitants have such a mixed heritage of natural characteristics. Perhaps the other species are . . . confused by the unconventional look of your species and choose to call out your extraordinary differences instead of learning to embrace them."

Tambreet looked past her wide, flat snout, down to the long claws extending from her wide, flat feet, then to her finely fur-covered paddle-like tail. She knew her species was unique among all the many reptiles, birds, and mammals. She even knew some juveniles seemed frightened of her, but the possibility of her natural *otherness* frightening both young and old of every species was an uncomfortable new concept for her.

A heaviness took up residence somewhere deep within Tambreet's chest. She looked to Counselor Corinna and said sadly, "But I cannot change my appearance. Does that mean I can do nothing to make friends with other creatures?"

Corinna knew then that her words had hurt Tambreet's feelings, even though she had only spoken the truth. Reaching out, the mermaid pulled the platypus to her in a gentle hug and softly said, "I am sorry. No, you cannot help your appearance. I, for one, would not want you to. I think you are perfect just the way you are, and I would like to be your friend."

Tambreet was grateful for the counselor's words. Yet, something still felt heavy within her. She had nothing to say. As the moon lit the shallow waters, Tambreet let the mermaid hold her.

And so Corinna held her.

After a little while, the counselor placed the juvenile platypus back upon the shallowly submerged rock. She studied her new young friend a little more closely. "You know," Corinna began again, with a twinkle in her eye. "I think I was wrong before."

The little platypus could see quite well in the dark and wondered what the mermaid's mischievous look meant. She waited for the counselor to continue. When she did not, Tambreet asked, "Wrong about what?"

"I was wrong when I said you had a beak that looked like a duck," Corinna continued. "Your snout is a perfect platypus snout, and *only* a platypus snout. Its soft texture and flexible nature make it the perfect tool to root for your food in the mud and soft sediments beneath the water."

Tambreet tried to look at her soft, leathery snout, which was hard to do since her eyes were set along its top edge. She thought about how the many tiny sensors in her snout told her where the shrimp or the worms were, no matter how dark the waters. She realized that without this sensitive snout, she would have a hard time finding food.

"You must be brave enough to keep trying to make friends," Corinna told her seeker. "Your species is an important part of our community. It is a pity the other youngsters cannot see this truth. Remember, just because you have not found very many kind creatures does not mean there are no kind creatures to be found. Keep being your sweet, friendly self, and I am certain you will eventually find genuine friends."

These hopeful words made Tambreet smile, and the heavy feeling inside her began to lighten.

Corinna smiled too. "Tambreet, I am sorry if others may see you as strange, but please remember that their perception of you is just that—a perception. The thoughts and opinions of others do not automatically make something true. The truth is *within* you, and what matters is staying true to yourself. You are a uniquely beautiful young platypus, an important member of our ecosystem, and I encourage you to embrace that as you continue to make friends with every species."

Tambreet needed another hug. In the darkness of night, she surprised Corinna by snuggling her soft, furry head underneath the mermaid's chin.

Corinna was happy to wrap her arms around Tambreet once again. Corinna held her tight and stroked her soft back. "You are enough, Tambreet. You have not been doing anything wrong in your attempt to make friends. Keep being kind to any creature who looks friendly and you will succeed. I know you will."

"Thank you for your honesty with me," the young platypus said. "Thank you for your friendship and this wonderful hug. I will tell my sister and brother the truth about what you said. It will be good for us to know it is not impossible to make friends with other species, for I have made a friend with a mermaid tonight."

Corinna smiled. "No, it is not impossible, my dear friend."

CHAPTER 4

ONE WARM, SUNNY MORNING, as had happened several times before, a new reptile came to speak with Counselor Tonino and ask his opinion on a matter.

When it was his turn, an old green and black iguana named Matlal (which means "dark green" in Nahuatl, the ancient language of the Aztec) ignored the connecting sand berm and swam out to the Guidance Rocks with the help of his powerful striped tail to approach the river otter. He climbed out of the water and onto a lower portion of the stone before introducing himself. "Good morning, Counselor Tonino. I am very pleased to meet you on this beautiful day. I am called Matlal."

"It is indeed a fine day, Matlal. I am pleased to meet you." Tonino paused to scratch an ear with his hind leg before continuing. "What is on your mind today?"

"Well, I am not sure how to begin."

"A good place to start is usually at the beginning," Tonino offered, grinning his toothy otter grin.

"Too true, too true." The iguana grinned back, the best an iguana can. "All right then. Yesterday began like any other, with the sun warming my favorite rock on the beach. As I lay there, eyes closed, I heard a faint scrabbling noise. I opened my eyes to see a young striped forest gecko staring at me. I asked her what she was doing, and she said she was basking in the sun, too. When I gently informed her that she was on my rock and asked her to vacate, she said, 'It is *a* rock, not *your* rock. You cannot claim a beach rock.' Then, I kindly shared how I have been sunbathing on that very chunk of stone every morning since I can remember; therefore, it *might as well* be my rock. But she did not like my words. She left in quite a huff. And yesterday afternoon I spied her sitting on my rock anyway, so I had to run her off."

Counselor Tonino nodded his furry otter head. "I understand. So, are you here to discuss her reaction or your own?"

The old iguana looked perplexed. "Whatever do you mean?"

From Matlal's confused response, Tonino was sure he knew the answer, so he tried a different approach. "You told a good story, but you did not ask me for advice."

"Oh. Yes, well." the reptile sounded flustered, and his head was now bobbing up and down. "I was wondering how to let the gecko know that I have staked a claim on that beach rock. I do not want her on it. Ever."

How does one live so many years without learning how to share? Tonino thought to himself. Though the river otter had no family (his parents and siblings had died when he was young), he knew his precious few possessions were still more than some creatures had. And a beach rock was the last thing he would choose to quibble over since there were so many to choose from. "Matlal, it seems as if you do not want anyone except yourself to set foot on this one specific rock."

"Yes, that is it. I do not want anyone else on the rock. It is mine and youngsters should have respect for their elder's wishes."

The river otter had to resist the urge to shake his head disapprovingly at the iguana. Tonino needed more information. "Okay. In regards to this one specific stone—have you made your home beneath it?"

"No, my burrow is in the seawall, near the trees. Everyone knows this. And everyone knows that rock is my sunbathing rock. It has always been mine."

"So no one has made a home either on top of or underneath it?"

Matlal had a sinking feeling this meeting was not going as he had hoped. "Yes, the rock is on a public beach, but that stone should be mine because I have used it after breakfast every morning for *years*. All my neighbors know this, except for the new ones and the young ones."

Tonino hoped that getting Matlal to say this out loud would help the iguana understand that he did not have a case. But the iguana's posture showed that he was as resolute as before, so the river otter offered a new option to Matlal. "Since you love this one rock so much, why do you not make your home underneath it? Then everyone would know the stone was the roof of your home and not bother you or the stone."

The old green and black iguana did not like that idea. He shook his head and flared the soft dewlap under his chin until it stood out. "I do not feel I should have to move my home from the seawall with all the other iguanas when everyone should already know the rock is mine."

"I see. Now these new neighbors do not know the sunning rock is yours alone—even when you are not using it—and you want me to tell them to stay off of it, yes?"

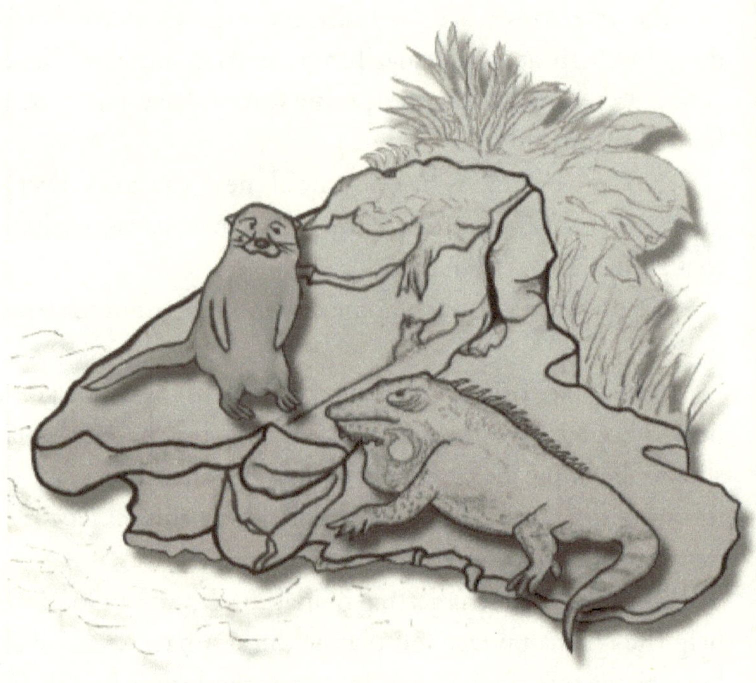

Matlal let the dewlap relax under his chin once more. The counselor was finally understanding him. "Exactly! That would be wonderful."

Tonino finally shook his head. "No. I will not do so, Matlal."

The iguana was confused. "But why?"

"The nature of community areas is to allow the public to enjoy all aspects of a place. If a dragonfly lands on the stone, would you chase it away?"

"No, that would be silly."

"Yet, when a young gecko sits on the stone, you chase her away."

"Yes, because it is not the same. A gecko is not a dragonfly. She is a fellow creature of the rainforest and a trespasser."

"She cannot trespass if the place is available for community use and not a home. I apologize, Matlal, but I cannot help you with the sunning rock, because you do not have a case."

The old green and black iguana stared at the river otter, trying to make him uncomfortable, and even flared his dewlap once more. He hoped this display of power might cause the counselor to change his mind.

But Tonino stared back and did not blink.

It turned into a silent, staring contest.

Finally, Matlal could stand it no longer. His patience was not what it once was. "Why will you not respect the opinion of your elder? I am many moons older than you; in fact, I remember the early spring day when you were born. I remember the day your family died while you were away, and the kind old mink couple who took you into their burrow. I bet if *they* asked you to keep something like a squirrel out of their home, you would help them."

The old iguana's speech shocked Tonino, but he did not break eye contact. Matlal's comparison was not really comparable, and he did not like being reminded of the day his parents and siblings died. It took all of his willpower, but Tonino successfully withstood the urge to say, *How dare you?*

Instead, the river otter calmly took a deep breath and slipped off of Guidance Rock and into the calm water of the estuary. He needed a moment to settle down, to let his muscles release their tension before he said something he would regret.

Matlal was surprised when the counselor dove into the water. When Tonino's head surfaced, the iguana watched the otter swim around the rock, once, twice, thrice, before returning to his place upon the boulder. Tonino shook his dripping body and the brief spray of brackish water showered the iguana. "What did you do that for?" Matlal asked indignantly.

"I simply needed to cool off. A dip every now and then is just the thing."

"Fine." Matlal answered curtly, though he was glad he won the staring contest.

"The fact remains, Matlal, that the sunning rock you are so protective about is considered community property unless someone makes a home either above or beneath it. I cannot help you stake a claim without your choice to move there. I can, however, help you find a way to share it."

"But I should not *have* to share it, everyone knows—"

"Yes, yes, everyone knows it is yours," Tonino interrupted. "Except—it is not yours and never has been." The river otter stopped to scratch his ear again, dislodging a water droplet that was tickling him. "I am sorry, my friend, but seekers such as yourself come and go, and families move from area to area around the lagoon. Your neighbors change, and not everyone is aware of your long-standing choice to sun on one particular rock."

The iguana huffed.

"So I suggest you either choose to dig a burrow under the rock, have a primate break it in half so you each get your own piece of stone, or choose to share the rock with this young gecko. Those are your only choices."

When Matlal opened his mouth to protest, Tonino held up a paw to stop him. "If we cannot change our circumstances, we must choose to change ourselves. The sunning rock is community property. Do you understand?"

The old green and black iguana stared at the river otter once more, hoping the counselor would change his mind.

This time, Matlal was the one who had to blink first, since a fly landed on one nostril and distracted him. He sighed in resignation. "Fine." The old iguana sighed. "I see your point, Counselor Tonino. I will not move my home from the seawall to the beach, because it is too far from the trees. And I will not break the best sunning rock on the beach in half, so I will choose to share with others." Matlal sighed again, knowing deep down that this was the right thing to do, but he did not like it, not one bit.

Tonino smiled his toothy otter smile and squeaked in excitement. "Good choice, my friend. You know, choosing to be flexible is the key to happiness. Perhaps I will sunbathe near you and the rock this week."

"Well, I guess I would like that," Matlal said.

Tonino knew the old iguana's improved attitude would affect everyone on the beach and perhaps motivate them all to have kinder hearts.

CHAPTER 5

THEN, ONE DECIDEDLY UNFORGETTABLE MORNING, a group of tidal area creatures had their chance to speak with the river otter at Guidance Rocks. A noisy flock of flamingos, who had been feeding nearby while they waited, came shuffling over as one enormous bunch. They squawked and honked amongst themselves as their heads bobbed and weaved to and fro. The spirited energy of the mass of pink and black feathers drew the attention of everyone nearby.

A brightly colored macaw had been conferring with Counselor Corinna, but the flamingo's commotion disturbed her. The macaw cut the conversation short and flew away quickly to find a quiet spot to rest in the rainforest.

Corinna could not help but notice the disturbed flock and signaled her helper to wait before bringing the next seeker to her. She usually used this signal when she wanted a break to go for a quick swim, but this time she wanted to see what the flamingos were so upset about.

Corinna turned to Tonino and raised her eyebrows to ask him a silent question.

The river otter understood what she was asking and nodded his agreement.

They would speak to this flamboyant flock of birds together. Tonino spoke first. "My friends! Please quiet down."

The honking and flapping lessened but did not completely subside. The shallow waters where they stood were turbulent with the throng's constant shuffling. Apparently, the birds in the back did not hear the river otter's message through their panicked shouts of, "They are coming!" and "No one is safe from these monsters," and "You have to help us!"

Tonino stood on his hind legs, using his long tail for balance. He stretched as tall as he could, and shouted, "Please! One at a time!"

By now, the chaotic ruckus had disturbed every lagoon inhabitant within hearing distance of the Guidance Rocks. They stopped what they were doing and turned to listen in on the forthcoming conversation.

The tall-legged birds finally settled into a shifty, uncomfortable kind of silence. They no longer spoke amongst themselves, but shuffled nervously in place, looking this way and that.

"Thank you," the river otter said gratefully. "Now—what seems to be the problem?"

After several false starts, a flamingo stepped forward as an impromptu spokesbird. "It is the humans," she said. "They are a threat to the entire Tidal Realm. Why, just the other day—"

But she was cut off when a shorter flamingo stepped out of the huddle and said, "You have to do something!"

An old one shouted, "They are becoming too numerous to ignore!"

Then another and another stepped forward and shared their news until most of the flock was once again flapping their pink and black wings and speaking all at once.

Tonino glanced at his fellow counselor and shrugged his little otter shoulders before sitting down once again. He shook his head, an exasperated look on his face.

Corinna the mermaid smiled at him. The noisy birds did not bother her. In fact, she thought the chaos was energizing. She winked at the river otter and took a deep breath of air before turning to slip into the shallow water. There was just enough space for her to swim into the forest of skinny flamingo legs and aim for the center of the group. Then she opened her mouth and sang. Her mermaid song calmed all those who listened to it, though the tall birds were too frantic to notice. Ultimately, it was the bubbles that got their attention. The escaping air tickled their sensitive legs and caused them to pause their panicked chatter and look down to the surface of the water.

Tonino took this quiet opportunity to bellow, "What about the humans? Have they interfered with your flock?"

The flamingos turned their now-quiet gaze from their submerged feet to the river otter. The spokesbird stepped forward again and answered, "Yes, that is what I said. I have heard they are becoming bold and are bothering nesting sites far inland, near the mountains."

"No, no," said a taller flamingo. "I heard they have taken over some coastal nesting grounds entirely and ate all the eggs left behind."

A flamingo from the back yelled, "That is not it!" The flock quieted as they made their way through the group to the front to speak. "The humans only scared off a bunch of egrets around the corner from the lagoon, no egg-eating was done at all."

"Wait, *humans*?" said yet another from the far back, raising his neck higher. "I thought the problem was *toucans*!"

This got the feathered group talking over each other once again, either agreeing with or correcting the last speaker's statement.

Corinna reemerged from the water, her scales glittering in the sun, and rolled her eyes at the noisy birds. She moved quickly back to the safety of the boulder as one flamingo after another stepped forward. The entire flock was jostling to the front of the crowd to share their truth.

It was not long before Corinna and Tonino were completely enveloped by panicky pink birds.

Tonino rubbed his head vigorously, trying not to get even more frustrated, before looking at his fellow counselor and sighing. "What shall we do?" he asked her quietly, scowling.

The flamingos continued their protest, not noticing the counselor's conversation. They were all busy talking *at* the counselors.

Corinna shrugged her bare shoulders, looking nonplussed. After gathering her thoughts, the mermaid replied to the river otter. "Apparently, the humans are growing in number more rapidly than we had considered. They must be encroaching very close to our protected lagoon to cause this much gossip."

"At the moment it is all hearsay, not to mention the many differing stories. Maybe we should send out an investigative party to find out the truth," he offered.

"I agree," answered the mermaid. "But we need to get this flock's attention again. I am not sure the bubbles will work a second time."

Tonino held up a paw. "No worries. I have an idea."

This time, the river otter slipped off the boulder and navigated carefully through the tall flamingo legs toward shore.

Corinna watched as Tonino re-emerged beyond the restless crowd, reached the shore, scampered across the beach, and disappeared into the dense foliage of the rainforest. She wondered what the clever little otter had in mind.

CHAPTER 6

MEANWHILE, HAMZA THE GREAT WHITE PELICAN watched The Tidal Realm's protected lagoon from up above, tilting his long wings occasionally to maintain the right altitude and position. The mass of moving pink feathers and black bill-tips below had his attention, too. Their noisy honking carried all the way to him on the coastal breeze.

An iridescent green and blue hummingbird named Kindi-Utkay (which means "rapid hummingbird" in Kichwa, the ancient language of the Incas) hovered near Hamza. He watched a nearby flock of starlings as he awaited instructions, his tiny feathers glinting in the sun. When the pelican caught his eye, the little bird zoomed closer and said, "Yes? Have you seen something? Do you have a message for a counselor?"

"No, actually," Hamza replied. "I was hoping you could fly down there and ask one of them what the commotion is all about. I have not seen this many upset flamingos since the nest-devastating flood incident a few years back."

"Me neither. Good idea. I will ask and be right back."

Kindi-Utkay dove quickly toward Guidance Rocks, and the cacophony of the flamingos grew louder as he flew over a cattail-choked corner of the lagoon. He reached the counselors just as Tonino slipped into the water and began swimming toward the beach alone. Instead of trying to have a conversation with the swimming otter, the hummingbird redirected his flight toward the mermaid. He zoomed twice around Corinna's head before landing on a small bit of rock poking out of the water next to her. He glanced toward the mass of agitated head-bobbing, wing-flapping birds before turning to the mermaid.

"Counselor Corinna," he twittered. "What is going on? What are these birds upset about?"

"Hello, Kindi-Utkay," she said, glad to see the speedy little bird. "It seems this noisy flock has heard a few differing rumors about encroaching human beings. We are unsure what the truth is since there is more than one version."

"Ah, yes. Information carried through many voices can become muddled. Is there a plan to learn what is truly happening?"

"I believe Tonino has something in mind, but he has not shared it with me just yet."

As a fresh sea breeze blew across the protected cove, Corinna's purplish-blue hair obscured her view of the hummingbird. She plucked the decorative shell from the side of her head, twisted her hair into a knot at the nape of her neck, and secured it in place with the same shell. "There, now I can see without my hair bothering me. It is so much easier underwater, where my hair flows around my head gracefully."

"I am certain it looks lovely underwater," Kindi-Utkay trilled. He fluffed up the feathers on his tiny hummingbird breast and turned toward the sun. "Does your hair shimmer underwater, like my feathers do in the sunlight?"

Corinna smiled. "I am not sure, my friend, since my eyes cannot see the back of my hair, but . . ." She paused to flick her long mermaid tail before continuing, "my scales gleam like your feathers are right now."

The little bird was proud that he had something in common with the counselor and fluttered happily. "I like that we have something in common," he trilled, though he was secretly grateful he had soft, light feathers instead of hard rough scales.

"Me too," Corinna said with a grin. "We also both enjoy adventuring and singing. How fun is it that we are both so different, yet so similar?"

Just then, Kindi-Utkay spotted Tonino swimming toward them. "He is coming back. We shall know his plan soon."

Corinna turned her gaze to the shoreline but did not see Tonino. Instead, she saw the tall trees near the shore swaying as if there were a strong wind. Then the guttural growling began.

At first, it was hard to hear over the noise of the panicked flamingos. But when the birds finally heard the ruckus, they quieted and turned to look at the distant tree line. Black and golden shapes emerged from the green of the forest's edge and perched in the trees. It was the howler monkeys.

"What are they doing?" asked Kindi-Utkay.

"Tonino must have asked the monkeys to get this panicked flock's attention," Corinna said with an amused smile. "Their loud guttural growling seems to have redirected the birds' focus."

As the howling died down, Tonino's head appeared near the counseling area. With his low otter-profile, it was difficult to see him. He climbed out of the water and shook violently, smiling mischievously when his cast-off water droplets made both the mermaid and hummingbird squeal.

Without giving time for the flamingos to resume speaking, Tonino turned and addressed the crowd, "Thank you for making us aware of a potential new threat to our lagoon. Since it is unclear if there are intruders, Counselor Corinna and I will send an investigative party to learn what they can firsthand."

The flamboyant flamingos honked and flapped their pink and black wings in cacophonous agreement. As usual, once they got going, it was hard for them to stop.

The river otter turned to the hummingbird. "I am so glad you are here, Kindi-Utkay. Can you please go tell the troop of monkeys to howl again?"

He dipped his head in a deferential bow. "It will be my pleasure," he said before flying off in a flash.

Corinna smiled at Tonino. "The monkeys were a great idea. We should remember this for the future."

Since hummingbirds are one of the fastest creatures in the sky, the counselors were not surprised when the monkeys began their growling almost immediately.

Once again, the deep, reverberating sound got the flamingos' attention. They stopped their chatter and gave their collective attention to the mermaid and the river otter.

Tonino continued. "Can one of you please step forward and tell us which direction this rumor came from? We need to know where to send the explorers."

Half of the crowd began speaking at once. "The humans are coming from the coastal flower fields on the sunset side," and "They are attacking from the mountains where the bitter wind blows."

These two places, of course, were not at all in the same direction. The counselors needed to narrow it down to one route.

Kindi-Utkay the hummingbird returned from his task and landed next to the mermaid once again.

Corinna nodded her head in a silent thank you to the little bird before turning back to the flamingos. She held up her hand and—miraculously—the flamboyant flock quieted down. "Thank you," she said. "Now, for those of you who heard that the humans are coming from the flower fields, please step to your left. If you heard humans are coming from the mountains, please step to your right."

The tall birds immediately began to move. They shuffled to either one side or the other, heads held high.

Corinna and Tonino could not tell which of the two groups was larger from their vantage point. The mermaid turned to Kindi-Utkay and said, "Can you please fly over the two clusters of birds and count the number in each group?"

"Yes, of course." Kindi-Utkay zoomed above the first cluster, hovering, counting, before moving over to the other group. He was glad to be so helpful to the counselors, but remembered he needed to get back to Hamza the pelican and report what he had learned.

This thought distracted him, and he had to count the second group again before speeding back to Guidance Rocks.

"There are thirty-three birds in the group closest to shore and thirty-nine in the other," Kindi-Utkay reported. After the mermaid and the river otter both thanked him for the information, he asked, "May I return to the watch commander now?"

"By all means," replied Corinna.

"We appreciate your help," said Tonino with a toothy otter grin. "May we consider you as a potential member of the exploration group?"

"Yes, of course. I would be honored," Kindi-Utkay sang, then bowed once more and launched into the sky to report back to Hamza.

CHAPTER 7

ONCE KINDI-UTKAY FLEW AWAY, Tonino addressed the flamingos again. "It seems you are divided nearly in half about which direction the humans are. Since a few more of you heard they are near the flower fields on the sunset side of the lagoon, we will send the investigators in that direction first."

The half of the flock that was certain the humans were encroaching from the mountains protested. But the mermaid held up a hand and they reluctantly quieted down.

"We know some of you are concerned that we may send explorers the wrong way," Corinna said. "Rest assured, if they find nothing near the coastal flower fields, we will send another group toward the mountains."

Again, half of the flamingos protested, but Corinna spoke loudly over them. "Thank you for coming to us and making us aware of the situation. Tonino and I will take it from here."

Tonino stood up on his short river otter hind legs and said, "We promise to keep everyone informed, since this is a potential threat to the entire community. We give you our thanks for bringing this to our attention. You are dismissed."

The flamboyant flock of flamingos took to the sky, honking noisily amongst themselves. as they returned to their nesting grounds.

Tonino turned to the nearby lagoon watchers. "Friends, please give us a little time to put together an investigative party before we resume our normal counseling activities."

The watchers nodded and turned to placate the grumbling creatures who were still waiting in line to talk with the mermaid and the river otter.

The tidal realm counselors turned to each other and spoke in low tones, so as not to be overheard.

"Who are you considering for the exploration team?" asked Tonino.

"Hmm. I think the hummingbird is an excellent idea. He can fly up high and keep a protective lookout around the others, as well as move quickly to send reports back to us."

"Agreed," said the river otter. "Speaking of protection, we should choose a fierce species, too. How about a crocodile? They can travel by water or land and have powerful jaws."

"I think a crocodile could be a good choice, even at their sluggish pace," answered Corinna. "Speaking of which, I think we should choose one or two who are swift on land. Perhaps a horse or a large feline?"

Tonino nodded. "Yes, I like both those ideas. How about sending Daithí the shaggy horse and Saphka the saber-toothed cat? The big cat can replace the crocodile since he is more agile on land, but then, who shall we send to explore the water along the way?"

Corinna knew just the person. "Might I suggest my husband, Zamir? Though he cannot travel overland, he and I have a strong mind-to-mind connection. He can travel parallel to the land party, staying in the shallow waters near shore. This would allow Kindi-Utkay to give him updates without the need to fly all the way home each time. Zamir can share any news with me immediately."

"That is a *great* idea," Tonino said. "Sometimes I forget about your species' special ability. How far are you able to reach other merfolk's minds?"

"I am unsure of the exact distance, but I am certain we can communicate as far as the coastal flower fields."

"Fantastic." Tonino stood and rubbed his front paws together in excitement. "I think we have chosen well."

"I agree," Corinna said with a smile. "Should we have a lagoon watcher call each of them to the beach? We must ask if they are willing."

The river otter almost nodded, but something else occurred to him. "Wait. I think we should choose a member of the evening patrol to keep tabs on the others as they sleep."

"Oh, yes, a good idea."

"How about a small white fruit bat?" Tonino suggested. "I have heard they like to adventure. Plus, they can roost during the day while holding onto the horse's long mane."

"Hmm," Corinna mused. "I am not sure their species is comfortable roosting anywhere besides underneath broad tree leaves. I doubt they could sleep under a moving lock of hair."

"Oh, good point. Well then, perhaps a bush baby? Might one of them be able to sleep while riding the saber-tooth or the horse?"

"Hmm. Not a bad idea." Corinna combed her hair with her fingers thoughtfully before speaking again. "How about Njool-Bët the bush baby and her twin sister, Nagapie? They are inseparable."

"Wonderful! I think we have our group," the river otter said, rubbing his front paws together once again. He was quite pleased by the diverse band of capable creatures they had selected.

Corinna gathered the waiting lagoon watchers and asked them to find the chosen daytime nominees. The counselors wanted to have them on the beach together for a conference, all except Zamir. Corinna would ask her husband herself, face-to-face.

The watchers departed immediately, each headed to find their assigned member of the investigative party.

Since it was shaping up to be a warm summer day, both of the counselors slipped into the cool water for a relaxing break. Soon after, Corinna told her fellow counselor she was going to swim home and ask her husband if he would join the expedition.

Tonino nodded his agreement. He swam a few lazy laps around the lagoon boulders while waiting for the first potential travelers to arrive on the beach.

The mermaid used her powerful tail fluke to hurry across the shallow waters. When she reached the long line of submerged sandbars, she dove straight for home. As she swam, she projected her thoughts toward her husband. *I am coming, husband. I am going to ask if you are willing to go on a special mission.*

Interesting, he answered. *You can find me working at the neighborhood farm today.*

Corinna arrived shortly after and they embraced tightly as they swam in a happy pirouette, tails entwined. "Zamir, it is so fun to see you in the middle of my workday," she said. "Are you able to talk about the mission as you tend the plants?"

"Yes, my dear, of course." He kissed her before returning to his task. "What is the purpose of this special mission?"

Corinna settled gently on the sandy floor to observe his trade. The current moved his medium-length green-blue hair gently back and forth in rhythm with the seaweed and kelp plants he worked alongside. After a moment of simply watching him, she finally answered. "You will soon hear rumors of humans encroaching near our sanctuary. I believe it might be true, but I am unsure. Tonino and I are planning to send an expedition team toward the coastal flower fields to discover the truth."

"Humans? Creatures that look like us on the upper half but walk on two legs? I have never seen one before. I always assumed they were a land-legend of some kind."

"Many of the inhabitants of Counselor's Cove believe that. We have been sheltered from much outside of this comfortable space over the ages. If this rumor is true, it might be time to fortify our protected borders. But first, we must verify the veracity of this report. Tonino and I would like you to be a member of the investigative party."

His brow furrowed in confusion. "Why me? You know we cannot travel on land for long distances."

"Yes, yes, please let me explain."

After Corinna laid out the details of her long-distance communication plan, Zamir smiled. "This is a clever idea, my dear. I officially agree to join the exploration team. I look forward to hearing more details over our evening meal together."

Once again, the newlyweds embraced tightly. Zamir pulled back and held Corinna at arm's length to tell her something he told her every day. "I am proud of the way you lead our community."

She answered as she always did. "Thank you, my love. I am proud of the way you feed our community."

Zamir grinned. "I hope this conversation never gets old."

Corinna grinned back, kissed him, and bade him goodbye before swimming back to the river otter and her duties.

CHAPTER 8

CORINNA RETURNED TO THE GUIDANCE ROCKS about the same time a coastal messenger parrot arrived with an update.

"The potential team members are assembled on shore and are awaiting word from you," she said.

"Thank you, we shall speak with them now," the river otter answered. He dove deftly into the lagoon and Corinna followed him to shore.

When the counselors arrived at the wide beach, the mermaid sat on the fine sand with her tail in the gently lapping water. Tonino stood on his hind legs among the land-dwellers, using his tail for balance. However, before he had a chance to address the group, the short, shaggy horse spoke up.

"What is all this about blood-thirsty humans and a possible invasion?" whinnied Daithí (which means "swift or nimble" in Old Irish).

The hummingbird, who was perched proudly on the horse's forehead, said, "Now, now, let the counselors share what they will before we get ourselves confused."

Corinna smiled at him in thanks and he fluttered his tiny wings in response.

"Thank you, Kindi-Utkay," Tonino continued. "Yes, there is a rumor that humans have ventured near this protected lagoon, but it is only a rumor. The report from the flamingos was unclear and they were divided on the direction of this possible threat. Counselor Corinna and I have decided to send a team toward the coastal flower fields first. We want you to join this team. We need members who will be cautious and not approach any humans, but travel quietly and learn what they can. If there is no noticeable human presence amongst the flowers, we will send a group toward the mountains."

"So, you need us to find out the truth," growled Saphka the somber saber-toothed cat (whose name means "knife" in Seminole). "I am not afraid of puny, fleshy humans. I accept this mission."

The hummingbird trilled his agreement without hesitation.

But, Daithí the shaggy horse nickered nervously to the saber tooth and said, "I will go if you promise to keep your teeth to yourself."

"Of course," Saphka answered. "I am not a heartless beast. On my honor, I promise not to harm my fellow travelers."

"Then I will go, too," Daithí said reluctantly. It was clear he was still nervous to be paired with a top predator, but he also understood the need for his protective presence.

"Excellent," Tonino said. "Now, you three represent only half of the group we would like to send." He turned to the mermaid, inviting her to share the rest of the plan.

"Yes," Corinna said. "Since we expect the trip to take a few days, we will send at least one member of the evening patrol to accompany you and guard over you as you sleep each night. We plan to ask a pair of bush baby sisters this evening if they are interested. Since they are night-dwellers, they will need to attach themselves to one of your shaggy manes during the day so they can rest. Is that agreeable?"

Both the horse and the saber-tooth nodded.

"Thank you," the mermaid said. "We will also send my husband Zamir along, though he will follow your progress from the waters along the coast. Kindi-Utkay, we would like you to report anything you learn along the way to Zamir, who will share the information with me through our mind-to-mind connection."

"Yes, of course," the hummingbird replied.

"This is a good plan," Daithí the shaggy horse said. "The three of us can all move as fast as the wind, and Saphka's long, piercing teeth can help protect us."

"When do we leave?" the saber-tooth asked, as his shoulder muscles twitched. He was eager to venture so far along the coast, where he had not formerly had a reason to travel.

Tonino spoke up again, "We must wait until we talk with the bush baby twins tonight, but we ask you to return to this spot at first light, ready to leave. Thank you for your willingness to go on such a strange and uncertain mission."

The diverse trio of animals nodded and expressed their excitement over the upcoming trip. Then, they dispersed to tell their families and friends of their imminent journey.

By now, it was mid-afternoon. The mermaid and the river otter swam back to Guidance Rocks and resumed their daily counseling duties. They conferred with a depressed hippopotamus, a small flock of arguing sandpipers, three angry fiddler crabs, and several more troubled seekers. Then, the nocturnal animals came with their questions and problems.

While the mermaid spoke with a black-crowned night heron, a messenger summoned Tonino back to shore. It was time to talk to the bush baby sisters. Since most otters are active at night, his keen eyesight helped him spot the waiting pair on the lowest branch of a distant tree, even in the feeble moonlight.

When the small bush babies saw Tonino approach, they jumped down from the branch to greet him.

"It is nice to see you again, ladies," the river otter began, smiling at the twins' adorable natural look, all fuzzy gray fur and oversized eyes. "Has anyone informed you of the task for which you have been chosen?"

"Yes," answered Njool-Bët (a name that means "large eye" in Wolof, a native language of Senegal). She nodded and her tiny bat-like ears wiggled a little. "We agree and welcome this adventure."

"We would like to see humans for ourselves," added her twin sister, Nagapie (which is Afrikaans for "night monkey"). "We understand we will need to keep watch in the trees while the others sleep."

"Yes, please." Tonino was delighted that the entire selected group had decided to go. No substitutions would need to be made. "Sound the alarm if you see danger approaching during the night. You should be aware of one very important detail. In order to go on this expedition, you must cling to either a long horse's mane or a saber-tooth's short neck scruff during daytime travel. Is this still agreeable to both of you?"

"A saber tooth?" Nagapie asked, her large eyes somehow growing larger.

"Yes," Tonino answered. "We have asked Saphka to go along to protect the group from any danger. He has promised, on his honor, that he will not harm his fellow travelers."

The little primates looked at each other briefly before turning back to the river otter. "Yes, we agree," they answered in unison.

"Excellent," Tonino said.

THE NEXT MORNING DAWNED bright and clear. The night's high tide had washed the beach clean of the previous day's travel marks and plant debris.

All six members of the investigative party had arrived and were waiting on the shore for final instructions.

Corinna sat next to her husband and marveled at how this diverse group of animals could come together and embrace such a plan. After all, they were all so different and did not usually spend time together.

A large gathering of curious lagoon dwellers and visiting seekers gathered in the trees, on the beach, and in the water to watch the official send-off. The flamingos gathered close, muttering amongst themselves and clacking their beaks impatiently. They were anxious to know what was going on outside Counselor's Cove, as were many of the creatures gathered nearby.

The mermaid and the river otter quietly discussed a few last-minute decisions with the traveling team.

"Kindi-Utkay, remember that Zamir will be waiting for word from you at least three times a day," Corinna said to the hummingbird. "You are welcome to check in as often as you like, but do not miss the morning, midday, or end-of-day visits with Zamir. If you miss these appointments, we will assume something has gone wrong and send out search parties to find you."

"Yes, yes," the hummingbird answered. "I will not fail."

Tonino turned to the horse and the saber-toothed cat. "Remember, move as silently as you can through the forest and grasslands. When you arrive near the flower fields, look for cover.

Send Kindi-Utkay to look for a human presence. Do not let the humans spot you."

"I promise," answered Daithí and Saphka, who both looked very serious and very silly, since each had the fluffy ball of a bush baby attached to the long hair on their necks.

"And my sister and I will carefully watch over them at night," Njool-Bët said sleepily.

"Yes. May we rest now?" Nagapie muttered before yawning.

"Of course," Corinna said softly. The twins buried their faces into their hosts' hair to hide from the bright sun before the mermaid continued. "We wish you safe travels and an easy return. I look forward to hearing how the expedition is going." Then, turning to Zamir she added quietly, "You will be missed."

Zamir smiled and flapped his tail fluke in the shallow water. "We should only be gone for a few nights. I know you want to come too, but you have your duties here. You will be safe with our families."

Corinna nodded and leaned into his bare chest for a hug.

The river otter stood on his hind legs, clapped his paws, and addressed the entire crowd. "Soon we will know the truth about the rumors of humans near our protected estuary. Counselor Corinna and I ask you to hold back all questions until the exploration team returns with information."

There was a collective sigh of disappointment from the crowd.

"Rest assured, if there is any immediate danger, we will not keep it from you."

The crowd's low muttering created an unsettling drone before they all fell quiet again.

Tonino turned back to the six adventurers to give them a farewell blessing. "May your travels be swift and sure. May the sun shine on you and the rain refresh you. May you go in peace and return in good health."

CHAPTER 9

TWO FULL DAYS PASSED SLOWLY inside the protected cove as life returned to its familiar pattern. The mermaid and the river otter met with the seekers of The Tidal Realm, and Hamza the great white pelican watched the far horizon for his little hummingbird friend's return.

Corinna was understandably distracted. Her new husband was off on a grand coastal adventure without her and she missed him terribly. Thankfully, Zamir reached out frequently with his strong mind-to-mind connection to keep her updated. A few times she had to ask him to wait so she could advise the seeker before her.

Then—finally—the information they had been waiting for arrived.

Is now a good time, my dear? asked Zamir.

Corinna was thankful she had just finished counseling a socially awkward eel and was between seekers. She signaled her helper that it was time for a break, then dove off Guidance Rocks to converse with her husband in private.

Yes, good timing, my love. What is the latest news? Corinna asked as she swam.

Wonderful, Zamir thought back. *Kindi-Utkay has reported the sight of a single human male in the flower fields. He appears to be all alone, possibly ill, and maybe even injured. He has not moved since first spotted. The explorers want to get closer, but request permission before proceeding.*

Corinna was stunned by her husband's news. She stopped swimming, which caused her long hair to envelop her face. Once she disentangled herself, she responded. *I had not anticipated an injured human. I will need to confer with Tonino before I can offer guidance.*

The mermaid rushed back to Tonino to find him on the Guidance Rocks counseling a ring-tailed lemur. Jumping onto her boulder, she sat and waited patiently for them to finish.

The lemur soon said goodbye and leapt back to the tree-covered island in the middle of the lagoon along a shallow sand berm.

Corinna was finally able to relay all she had learned to the river otter. She finished with, "I believe we should help the poor man."

But Tonino was already shaking his head. "I do not see how we can help. We cannot communicate with him, we do not understand his needs, and we do not know how to help him heal. I think it is a dangerous idea."

The mermaid agreed with Tonino, but had a feeling deep down that they should try to help the injured human anyway. She was unsure how to make her case. "My friend," she began, hoping the right words would come to her, "I hear what you are saying and do not disagree. However, the exploration team feels strongly about trying to help the man, no matter the uncertainty or potential risk to themselves."

When Tonino opened his mouth to protest, Corinna rushed on. "Perhaps they can approach very slowly. We can give Daithí permission to get closer to the human. From there, his natural equine instincts should tell him if the man might be a threat or not. Then we can decide if the adventurous group should bring the human home."

The river otter closed his mouth and considered her comments before responding. "All right. Fine. I trust Daithí's instincts. However, they all must be *extremely* cautious."

"Yes, of course." Corinna was elated, yet still unsure why the issue had become so important to her. Trying to help the injured man simply felt like the right thing to do. She was grateful not to need to argue the point any longer. "Thank you. I will relay the information to Zamir now. Hopefully we will hear something back very soon."

The mermaid closed her eyes and reached out to her husband with her thoughts.

Tonino sat in awkward silence as he waited.

Finally, Corinna received a response from her husband.

I am told the human made no attempt to harm Daithí, but struggled to sit up and reach out an arm to touch the horse's mane, Zamir said. *It appears the man has dried blood all over both legs, and his strength is almost gone.*

The mermaid shared this news with the river otter, who felt immediate compassion for the injured human. "Very well. If the horse and the saber-toothed cat are willing, I agree to allow the man onto our protected shores. We can help with his wounds, but I am unsure how we may feed him. If he has indeed raided flamingo nests for eggs, he cannot be allowed to do so again. He will need to be content with whatever food we bring him."

"Agreed," Corinna said, grinning happily.

KINDI-UTKAY KEPT ZAMIR INFORMED every step of the way. Zamir shared the information with Corinna, who relayed it to Tonino.

Corinna described how Daithí the shaggy horse had knelt down next to the human in the flower fields and waited to see what the human might do. The sun was near the horizon by the time the man had progressed from gently stroking the horse's mane, to cuddling into his flanks for warmth, to following Daithí's gentle muzzle-prodding to climb onto his back. Once the human lay balanced on his back, Daithí carefully stood up and walked slowly back to the cover of the trees. Saphka waited for them in the shadows with the twin bush babies clinging to his neck. Upon seeing the saber-tooth, the human trembled, obviously terrified of the big cat.

"This puny creature looks near death," Saphka had said. "Should I kill him now and put him out of his misery?"

"No, no," Daithí had whinnied. "We are to take him to the counselors."

So the group began their journey back to the estuary. Daithí walked a few paces behind the saber-tooth as they started slowly toward home because the man was terrified of Saphka.

Inside Counselor's Cove that night, many interested inhabitants gathered together to hear the news from the mermaid and the river otter. Once the crowd of creatures was told the investigative party was returning with an injured human, their curious murmuring turned to sounds of panic.

The flamingos, in particular, erupted into chaotic squawking and wing flapping. They were not interested in helping a potential egg-eating monster recover. They shouted, "But what if it is a trick?" and "How many more are hiding close by?" and especially "You cannot bring a human here!"

One flamingo finally stepped forward as a spokesbird. "We should not allow this! Humans are *dangerous* and not to be trusted near our nesting flats, much less *here*, inside Counselor's Cove!"

This outburst was echoed by many and the crowd pressed forward, toward the submerged boulders where the counselors sat. Corinna waved a hand high in the air to signal the howler monkeys. The primates' loud guttural growling redirected their panicked attention, and they all settled back down into an anxious, shifting quiet.

Tonino stood on his hind legs, clapped his paws, and addressed the restless multitude again. "Friends, we should not let our fears rule us. We all know and love Daithí the horse. Counselor Corinna and I trust his instincts and ask that you choose to do the same. We do not believe Daithí would willingly carry a threat into our protected sanctuary. Remember, right now there is only *one* human, and he is far too injured to walk. If we can give him a safe place to heal—far away from any of our vulnerable offspring—why would we not?"

Many of those gathered spoke out simultaneously.

"Maybe we should restrain him!"

"This can only mean trouble."

"What if it is a trap?"

But soon the crowd quieted down once more.

Corinna took their near-silence as a good sign. "The exploration team has not seen any other humans on their trip—just the one. We do not think he is a part of a trap. We simply want to help him."

There were no outbursts this time and the river otter addressed them again. "Corinna and I will have a place prepared for the man to recover on the shore near these rocks. We will not allow him to wander freely. If any of you are uncomfortable with his presence, we ask that you avoid the area while the human recuperates. Go visit friends and family elsewhere, or keep to the other side of the lagoon, but do not harass the human."

The crowd shifted nervously, but did not erupt into chaos again. Even the flamingos did no more than clack their beaks in disagreement.

Corinna was pleased. "Thank you for trusting our decision and for your willingness to show a stranger compassion. Who knows? We may all learn something valuable from this human."

CHAPTER 10

HAMZA THE GREAT WHITE PELICAN watched the far horizon anxiously for the return of his hummingbird friend. He knew from other aerial messengers and lagoon watchers that the investigative party was on their way back with an injured man. He wanted to hear more details directly from Kindi-Utkay.

Hamza observed the beach as the watchers swept a shady spot clear of shells and other debris with sticks and branches. Volunteer chimpanzees brought fallen tree trunks from the forest and created a secluded circular space on the sand for the human to stay. They completed the private nest with a fresh pile of leaves to serve as a bed for the human.

Finally, Hamza saw movement in a small clearing in the rainforest. It was the shaggy horse and the saber-toothed cat, and there was a small crowd of forest animals following them at a distance.

The pelican called a nearby sparrow and asked, "Can you ask Kindi-Utkay to come speak with me as soon as he can?"

The little sparrow nodded and dove for the opening in the tree canopy. Not long after, Hamza heard the rush of tiny wings as the hummingbird approached.

"Hamza, Hamza, have you heard? A human is coming to the lagoon!"

"Yes, my friend. The man seems small laying on Daithí's back. Do you think our neighbors will welcome him?"

"We can only hope." the hummingbird answered breathlessly. "Now, I must go learn where the counselors have decided the man is to recover, so I can lead Daithí there."

"Yes, yes, of course. See you later," Hamza answered, though he knew the location of the human's nest.

Kindi-Utkay the hummingbird zoomed toward Guidance Rocks. Tonino appeared to be alone, so he landed next to the river otter.

"Why, hello there!" Tonino said in happy surprise. "I am glad to see you are back safely. Corinna and I have been waiting for your arrival. Where is the rest of the team?"

"They are nearby and should arrive shortly. Where are we to take the human? He does not seem well, no, not at all."

Just then, the mermaid finished speaking with a school of archer fish underwater and surfaced next to them. "Oh, welcome home, Kindi-Utkay," she said with a smile.

"Thank you. It is good to be back," the little bird answered.

"I was just going to show him the shady spot on the beach we have set aside for the man," Tonino said.

"Wonderful," Corinna said. "I will stay here and continue to meet with seekers."

"Thank you, my friend," Tonino said before he dove into the water. Then he surfaced and said to the hummingbird, "Follow me."

Kindi-Utkay flew above Tonino as he swam toward shore and to the log circle that had been prepared for the human.

"This looks perfect. I will bring Daithí right here," Kindi-Utkay said before zooming back to the investigative group.

Tonino inspected the spot one more time. The leafy pile looked soft and comfortable. There were no shells, sticks, or other objects to make it uncomfortable, or to be used as a weapon.

Not long after, the saber-toothed cat emerged from the rainforest, followed by the shaggy horse with his human burden. They slowly made their way across the beach to the little encampment. A large, curious crowd of birds and animals trailed behind them, though they were surprisingly quiet.

Tonino loped to the forest's edge to meet them. When he was near enough, he saw the man's bloodied legs dangling on either side of Daithí the horse. He felt a flood of compassion.

"He is asleep," Daithí said quietly. "He has refused any food but drank water from a stream last night. I am glad we are done traveling. I am afraid the human may not be able to hold on to my mane much longer. May we ask a few volunteers to help get him to the ground?"

Tonino nodded. "Yes, that is a brilliant idea." The river otter then asked the hummingbird to find any creatures willing to help.

"If you do not need me," Saphka said to Tonino, "I will take the bush baby twins home and meet you later."

"Good idea," the river otter said.

As they arrived at the human's beach nest, four male chimpanzees strutted up to the circle of fallen logs. The largest of the group, named Maseka (which means "laughter" in the

Kikongo language), approached Daithí. "We built this nest. We will help move the human and take care of his needs."

"Thank you," Tonino and Daithí both answered.

The semi-conscious human did not object to Maseka and his crew gently lifting him off Daithí's back. In fact, the man seemed unable to wake. The chimps carried him carefully over the logs and onto the soft pile of leaves, where he promptly curled into a ball and lay still.

The animals did not know much about human physiology, but they had a sense that his breathing seemed far too slow. Daithí the shaggy horse and the four chimpanzees stationed themselves around the encampment, and settled in to keep a quiet watch over the injured human. A female chimp came with a coconut half filled with water from the river and left it with Maseka.

A multitude of curious onlookers talked quietly amongst themselves. Tonino overheard things like, "This monster is faking and will eat us in our sleep tonight," and "It is such a weak-looking species," and "He looks so miserable, so harmless. I hope we can help."

The river otter let them have their mutterings. He turned to the shaggy horse and the chimpanzees. "This nest looks perfect," Tonino said. "Thank you for volunteering for such a strange and sensitive problem. I will bring Corinna over, and we will all see what we can do to help."

The chimpanzees showed their teeth politely in agreement and nodded a few times.

The river otter hurried back to the Guidance Rocks and waited for the mermaid to finish speaking with a pair of storks. He called her aside to inform her that the human was now settled inside the little log-ringed camp.

"Wonderful," she exclaimed. "I cannot wait to meet him."

Corinna and Tonino eagerly jumped into the water and swam to shore. Unfortunately, the counselors arrived just in time to watch him take one last, ragged breath.

The man was dead.

Corinna, Tonino, Daithí, and the chimps were stunned. They had all committed to helping the human heal from his injuries but were given no time to do so. Either they had been too late, or the two-day trip back to Counselor's Cove had been too much for his fragile body.

They would never know.

When some of the onlookers learned the human was dead, their curious murmuring turned to sounds of joy.

The flock of flamingos erupted into chaotic squawking and wing flapping. They were elated that the potential egg-eating monster had died. One flamingo stepped forward to speak. "Our nesting flats are safe! This human has gotten what he deserved and will not bother us anymore."

This outburst was echoed by many lagoon inhabitants and the crowd began to disperse.

Corinna was heartbroken. This was not how she had hoped things would turn out.

"Wait!" Tonino shouted. He stood on his hind legs, clapped his paws, and addressed the multitude again.

Many turned back to listen, though not all.

"Why are you so pleased?" the river otter continued. "We do not know if this injured human damaged the nests of our neighbors. There may yet be danger nearby. We should stay vigilant, just in case."

Those still present settled into an anxious, shifting silence. The tension was palpable.

"Friends, please choose not to be so quick to judge," Tonino continued. "At first I too was nervous when I heard about the man, but now I am saddened to lose this opportunity to meet a new species. I know we are wary of humans, and that may prove to be the correct feeling someday. But I was looking forward to helping this stranger."

The crowd muttered their various opinions on the matter.

The mermaid had been speaking mind-to-mind with Zamir, who was still swimming back to the estuary's sandbar entrance. They each grieved the man's death.

The mermaid and the river otter invited the community to pay their respects to the human. Maseka and his troop of chimpanzees continued their guard around the encampment. The lagoon inhabitants were curious and lined up to see the human. Some were deeply saddened by the death of the man, though more were unsure how they felt.

The counselors heard surprising whispers, things like, "He does not look bloodthirsty to me," and "He looks so small," and "He does not look like a monster."

As the procession dwindled, Tonino pulled Corinna aside. "What should we do about the body?"

The mermaid thought for a while but had no answers. She decided to reach out to Zamir with her thoughts. *My husband, have you made it home?*

Yes, he replied. *I have just arrived.*

So, Corinna asked for his opinion on the matter of the body.

It seems to me, Zamir answered, *that the top half of the human is similar enough to our species, that we could ask our people if they would be willing to give him a mer-burial.*

Corinna was surprised she had not thought of that herself. *Oh, wonderful! Yes, please see if you can arrange it with our elders. Thank you, Zamir. You are brilliant.*

Zamir blushed. She was always giving him compliments, but somehow they still took him by surprise. *Thank you, my dear. I will talk to you soon.*

Corinna turned back to her fellow counselor. "Zamir and I would like to give the human a mer-burial, if our elders are willing."

"That is a wonderful idea," Tonino said. "That would keep angry inhabitants like the flamingos from damaging his body."

So, Daithí the shaggy horse, Saphka the somber saber-tooth, and Maseka the chimpanzee stood watch over the human throughout the rest of the day. Before sunset, the mer-elders informed the lagoon counselors that they would be honored to give the body of the human to the sea. Corinna and Zamir led a pod of mermen to the circle of fallen logs, where they gently moved the human into the lapping surf. They wrapped the body in seaweed while Zamir sang a hauntingly beautiful song.

Hamza the great white pelican and Kindi-Utkay the hummingbird viewed from above as the merfolk carried the wrapped body with them into the deeper waters. The merfolk moved easily past the estuary's submerged sandbars and into the deep open ocean. The two birds watched until the deep blue of the waters swallowed the somber procession.

Hamza finally spoke. "I am sad that the human died before we could learn more about his species."

"Me too," answered Kindi-Utkay. "All we learned from the trip is that humans are just as fragile as we are. They bleed and die—just like us."

"Of that I had no doubt," the pelican said. "All living creatures have death in common."

"Yes, but I had heard rumors about humans having special abilities—magical abilities."

"We cannot believe every rumor we hear," answered Hamza. "We must remember to get the sky view—and not just the ground view—before choosing to believe a thing."

"True," the hummingbird sighed. "Many flamingos are still convinced humans are already a problem for The Tidal Realm. I wonder if we will find a way to live near each other someday."

"I hope so. Every species must find a way to exist with one another, though some relationships are more difficult than others," Hamza mused.

Kindi-Utkay agreed. "Yes, you are right. Maybe we can try to be better prepared for such an encounter next time. That may help us approach things differently."

Hamza contemplated this before he spoke again. "Our fears can run away with our senses and cause our words to multiply, until the thing we feared no longer resembles reality. It is especially difficult if we cannot see the sky view."

"It appears a life lived through a ground view is more difficult," answered Kindi-Utkay thoughtfully.

The two birds—one large, one small—continued to circle above Counselor's Cove. They allowed the silence to stretch between them, before Kindi-Utkay the hummingbird bid the white pelican a goodnight and flew home to his tiny nest. As the sun touched the horizon, and the hint of twilight descended, Hamza spied the wide wingspan of Lalita the large fruit bat. She was flying up from the mangrove forest to relieve him as watch commander for the night.

"Hello, Hamza." said the night patrol officer as she joined him in his aerial pattern above the cove. "I heard there was quite the excitement with the arrival and death of the human today."

"Indeed," Hamza said. "It was a sad day."

"Yes, it seems like a sad situation," Lalita answered somberly. "I am certain things will return to normal around here very soon. Life goes on."

"Unless it does not," Hamza said, eliciting a giggle from Lalita.

"True, true," she answered. "Now, go to bed, my friend. I will see you at dawn."

"Thank you. I will see you tomorrow." Hamza dipped his wings and made his way home, to his partner and his newly hatched chicks.

Soon, the nocturnal seekers would end their time with the counselors. The new day would dawn, and new creatures would once again approach Guidance Rocks to work out their concerns. But on this night, all was quiet in the realm of the mermaid and the river otter.

THE END

PRONUNCIATION OF CHARACTER NAMES

(in alphabetical order)

CHARACTER	ORIGIN	PRONUNCIATION
CORINNA the mermaid	Greek	kȯr-rin-nə (ko-RINN-nah)
DAITHÍ the horse	Old Irish	dȯ-hē (DAH-hee)
HAMZA the great white pelican	Turkish	häm-zə (HAAM-zuh)
KINDI-UTKAY the hummingbird	Kichwa, Ancient Language of the Incas	kin-dē-u̇t-kā KIN-dee-OOT-kay
LALITA the fruit bat	Sanskrit	lä-lē-tä (la-LEE-tah)
MASEKA the chimpanzee	Kikongo	mä-sē-kə (ma-SEE-kuh)

MATLAL the iguana	Nahuatl, ancient Aztec	mä-tläl (MAH-tlahl)
NAGAPIE the bush baby	Afrikaans	nȯ-gäp-ē (na-GAPE-ee)
NJOOL-BËT the bush baby	Wolof, a language of Senegal	n-yȯl-bət (nYOL-buht)
SAPHKA the saber-toothed cat	Seminole	saf-kə (SAFF-kuh)
TAMBREET the platypus	Indigenous Australian	täm-brēt (TOM-breet)
TONINO the river otter	Italian	tō-nēn-ō (toe-NEEN-o)
ZAMIR the merman	Hebrew	zä-mir (zah-MEER)

ACKNOWLEDGMENTS

M Y SINCERE THANKS TO YOU, MY READER, for your support of this fable. Without your interest, I would be merely telling stories to myself. My hope is that you've enjoyed this little book.

Thank you to my husband's parents, Junior and Kay, to whom this fable is dedicated. They've been supportive of my writing adventures from the beginning. My mother-in-law has been kind enough to listen to me for hours as I read my projects out loud. Her keen interest and gracious feedback have helped me feel more confident in my trade.

Once again, I want to thank my parents, Greg and Anne, for their unwavering interest in all my writings, and their proof-reading assistance. Their comments regarding each and every draft were extremely helpful. And thank you to my father in particular, for providing the animal sketches included in my fable series.

I would like to thank the helpful members of my writer's critique group: Barb, Barbara, Denise, and Pete. They were careful to pay attention to the intended voice of the story, and not try to make it sound like a commercial fiction project. Their offered suggestions helped to make this little fable even better, particularly regarding an earlier draft of the platypus chapter.

Thank you to my beta reader friends Wendi and Debby, who shared their helpful feedback quickly and happily. Their editing choices and clarity concerns were right on the nose, helping bring this story to its fullest potential.

I also need to thank my neighbors, Cyndy, Jeff, Nancy, Haley, Don, Pam, and Bill who have listened to me blather on about this project (and others), and still offered me their wisdom and advice.

And last, but certainly not least, I thank my husband, Eddie. Though fiction (and reading in general) are not his idea of a good time, he still supports me. He encourages me to keep pushing, keep learning, keep honing my craft—and that, my friends, is invaluable.

This fable is a much better story due to the honest feedback I've received from each and every one of these generous people. You've all made my writing journey a rich experience.

Thank you!

About the Author

CS Simpson is a multi-genre writer of several short stories, some poetry, and a novel. Her work can be found in Shoreline of Infinity, the Pikes Peak Writers Anthologies, frontiertales.com, and her own self-published fables. When she's not writing, editing, or stressing about writing, she's either devouring other author's books or playing The Sims and watching movies while sipping Diet Coke. She also enjoys short hikes with her husband and dog under the Colorado skies she calls home.

Keep up with her writing journey at www.authorcssimpson.com

Read more at www.authorcssimpson.com.